The RELUCTANT RAJPUT

Crabtree Publishing Company
www.crabtreebooks.com

PMB 16A, 350 Fifth Avenue,
Suite 3308,
New York, NY 10118

616 Welland Avenue,
St. Catharines, Ontario
Canada, L2M 5V6

For Christiane, Miriam and Melissa

R.M.

For Mum and Dad

D.D.

Cataloging-in-Publication data is available at the Library of Congress.

Published by Crabtree Publishing in 2006
First published in 2005 by Egmont Books Ltd.
Text copyright © Richard Moverley 2005
Illustrations copyright © David Dean 2005
The Author and Illustrator have asserted their moral rights.
Paperback ISBN 0-7787-2745-9
Reinforced Hardcover Binding ISBN 0-7787-2723-8

The RELUCTANT RAJPUT

WRITTEN BY
RICHARD MOVERLEY

ILLUSTRATED BY
DAVID DEAN

GO Bananas

Chapter One

"Now, children," said Mrs. Gupta. "Put your mathematics away and listen."

Bhupinder wiped clean his slate and put it down on the floor beside him. He glanced around the class. Thirty children of varying ages sat cross-legged, looking at their teacher. Mrs. Gupta stood at the front next to the blackboard. Near to her, a few books were on the floor. This was Nantapur village school, in Andhra Pradesh, southern India.

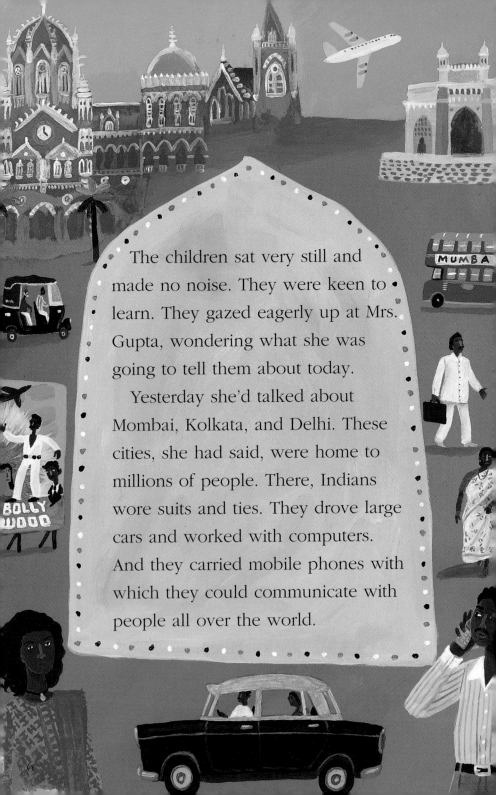

The children sat very still and made no noise. They were keen to learn. They gazed eagerly up at Mrs. Gupta, wondering what she was going to tell them about today.

Yesterday she'd talked about Mombai, Kolkata, and Delhi. These cities, she had said, were home to millions of people. There, Indians wore suits and ties. They drove large cars and worked with computers. And they carried mobile phones with which they could communicate with people all over the world.

For the children of Nantapur, it was hard to imagine. They didn't even have running water or electricity. And nobody owned a car. There was just an old bus. Often it was so full that you had to sit on the roof or stand on the steps. In Nantapur, roads were for walking.

Could it really be the same India?

Sometimes Bhupinder and his friends thought that Mrs. Gupta made these tales up. But they were better than having to do math!

"Today I want to tell you about Rajasthan," said Mrs. Gupta. "Rajasthan is a large state with some fabulous forts. It's about a thousand miles north of here. It hardly ever rains, so the land is very dry. But it's very colorful. And the women wear bright saris and lots of jewelry."

The girls smiled. They imagined themselves as Rajasthani princesses, living in fantastic fortresses and proud palaces. Wearing silk saris of salmon pink or scarlet.

Sky blue or sunshine yellow.

Lime green or lilac.

Then there was the jewelry. Gold bangles and bracelets. Gold necklaces and earrings. Gold nose pins and silver anklet chains. Chunky silver rings.

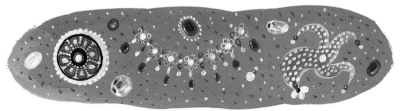

Bhupinder wasn't interested in clothes and jewelry. He gazed out at the small cluster of houses. He could see the young children playing, chasing chickens along the narrow muddy lanes. The old men were chatting in the village square. And the women were gathered around the well. They had come to fetch water in large brass pots, which they carried home balanced on top of their heads.

Bhupinder could almost see his family's small wooden hut. He could picture his sister Shaloka sitting on the porch, making butter with a clay pot and a long pole.

Farther away his father would be working in the rice fields on the edge of town. Mr. Chowdhury was a farmer. He worked barefoot in the swampy ground. He wore a cotton dhoti wrapped around his waist and a cloth around his head to mop up the sweat.

It was very hot in Nantapur! The sun
scorched down from a clear blue sky.
Sometimes it was hard to keep going,
never mind to work in the fields.

The worst, as Bhupinder knew, was just
before the monsoon. Then the whole village
was like a fiery furnace . . . Until, finally, the
monsoon rains fell – turning the village streets
into rivers of muddy water.

Bhupinder smiled to see a large cow waddle into one of the huts. As he watched, it suddenly stumbled against the wooden pole, knocking down leaves from the roof and making the whole hut shake. The villagers were Hindus, so cows were sacred to them. They could not be eaten or mistreated. They were almost like pets. Bhupinder's family owned a cow called Nandi. She was always waddling into the house, knocking things over and generally getting in the way.

Chapter Two

"The Rajputs were fierce fighters," said Mrs. Gupta. "They believed that they belonged to a special warrior caste and even fought battles against the armies of the mighty Moghul Empire."

Bhupinder stopped gazing around. He sat up straight and pricked up his ears. Mrs. Gupta was telling the class about the proud Rajputs, who built Rajasthan's colossal forts.

"They were fearless," she said, "even against overwhelming odds. If a battle was lost they marched out in their thousands to face almost certain death."

"Wow!" thought Bhupinder. "That's more like it."

"Which was the biggest fort?" he blurted out, unable to stop himself.

"Well I don't know for sure," admitted Mrs. Gupta, "but one of the largest and most extravagant was the Meherangarh, on the edge of the Thar desert at Jodhpur. And it's still there today!"

"Tell us about it," said Bhupinder. "Please!"

"Yes, yes, go on," shouted the other children. "What's it like? How big is it?"

"Well," said Mrs. Gupta. "The Meherangarh is

known as the Majestic
Fort. It was built on top
of sheer rock cliffs and
the walls are up to one
hundred and fifteen feet
high and sixty-six feet
wide."

"Go on, go on," yelled
the children.

"It has seven monumental
gateways," said Mrs. Gupta,
"and it is reached by a steep,
twisting path that was
designed to halt a charging
elephant. From here the
Rathore dynasty ruled
over Marwar, 'the Land
of Death' . . ."

"The Land of
Death!" Bhupinder's
imagination began to
run wild. He thought
of the glamour of

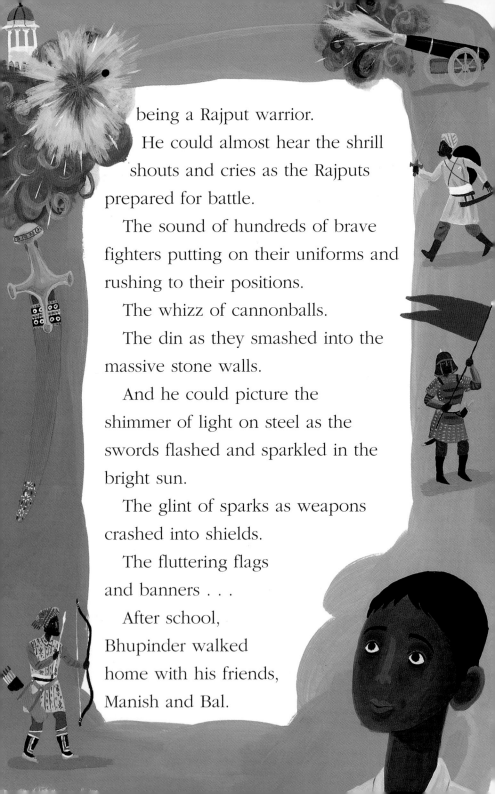

being a Rajput warrior.

He could almost hear the shrill shouts and cries as the Rajputs prepared for battle.

The sound of hundreds of brave fighters putting on their uniforms and rushing to their positions.

The whizz of cannonballs.

The din as they smashed into the massive stone walls.

And he could picture the shimmer of light on steel as the swords flashed and sparkled in the bright sun.

The glint of sparks as weapons crashed into shields.

The fluttering flags and banners . . .

After school, Bhupinder walked home with his friends, Manish and Bal.

The boys were too poor to own any toys. But they did have a battered old cricket bat. And a lumpy, handed-down ball that was almost egg-shaped and no longer rolled straight. Most nights after school they played cricket on a patch of wasteland on the edge of town.

But today they had other ideas.

"I want to be a Rajput!" said Bhupinder.

"So do I," yelled Manish.

"Me too," said Bal. "But who's going to be a Moghul?"

Nobody volunteered!

"I know," said Bhupinder. "Let's all be Rajputs."

"Good idea," agreed Manish and Bal.

The boys played at being Rajputs all the way home. They stood tall and tried to look frightening.

They let out blood-curdling cries.

They slashed out at imaginary enemies with imaginary swords.

They yelled with triumph as the enemy retreated, wounded and defeated.

And they argued about which of them was the bravest.

Which was the strongest.

Which was the most frightening.

Chapter Three

Eventually, Bhupinder reached home. His mother was cooking dhal and rice on a small mud stove in front of the house. Bhupinder could see the thin wisps of smoke rising from the fire. He poured a trickle of precious water into a small brass bowl, put in his hands and rubbed them together. Carefully, he washed off the day's dust and grime. Then he sat down with the rest of the family on the porch.

They all sat in silence, waiting for Mrs. Chowdhury to hand them a bowl of food. They ate with their hands. First they mixed some dhal with the rice. Then they squeezed it into tight balls with their fingers. And then they lifted it to their mouths . . . It tasted good!

After the meal, the children all had jobs to do. Shaloka sat on the porch, weaving clothes on a wooden loom. The older boys went to collect water from the well. And Bhupinder had to make "dung cakes." To the villagers of Nantapur, dung cakes were very important.

First Bhupinder
collected Nandi's
dung into heaps.
Then he mixed it
with straw and patted
it into "cakes". Finally
he slapped them
against the wall to dry

in the sun. After that they could be burned as
fuel for cooking.

But tonight, Bhupinder's mind was not on
the job. It was racing with thoughts of the
fierce Rajput warriors and their fantastic forts.
They lived a life of color and excitement.
Bhupinder's life seemed so boring in contrast.
Nothing ever happened in Nantapur. And there

was certainly nothing
glamorous about
making dung cakes!

If only he could be a
Rajput! How wonderful
that would be. A Rajput.
Just think . . .

Gradually, the wooden huts and rice fields dimmed. The smells of charcoal fires and boiling rice began to disappear. The hubbub of conversation and the shouts of children became muffled. Bhupinder closed his eyes and bowed his head.

Suddenly he slumped to one side. His chin fell against his chest. He was asleep!

Chapter Four

Bhupinder woke with a start and looked around him. He was all alone in a huge room with thick columns. It was filled with gold-encrusted swords and ornamental daggers. There were long pikes and suits of armor. Guns and cannonballs. Where was he?

He walked on.

The next room was just as large. The walls were covered with miniature paintings of gods and kings. There were large gilded mirrors and ornamental screens. Oil lamps shimmered from the ceiling. And there were great silk carpets and a large carved bed.

"I must be in a palace," thought Bhupinder.

He was right. He was in a palace. In fact
he was in the royal apartments of the
Meherangarh.

"Where is everybody?" thought Bhupinder.
He looked out across the courtyard. The fort
was huge. A higgledy-piggledly jumble of
battlements and lookout towers sprawled across
the rocky hillside. And the walls! They were
thicker than an elephant's hide. In parts they
were more than sixty-six feet wide.

But there were no people to be seen.
Bhupinder moved cautiously towards the
ramparts and looked down. The sheer drop
took his breath away. Below him he could see
the plains stretching far away into the distance.

Sounds drifted up from the narrow streets outside the walls. But they weren't sounds of craftsmen and conversation. There was something strange about them. Something discordant. They were sounds of shouting. Sounds of rumbling wheels and jangling metal. Sounds of horses' hooves and heavy boots. Sounds of . . . an army!

Bhupinder moved closer to the wall and peeped over. He couldn't believe what he saw. He rubbed his eyes and looked again. It was true. There, just below him, were the massed ranks of the Moghul army. There were thousands of them. And they were all armed to the teeth, their weapons polished and gleaming in the sun.

Chapter Five

"They must be planning a surprise attack," thought Bhupinder. "Where is everybody? How can I warn them?" He rushed back into the palace and ran quickly from room to room. "Moghuls! Moghuls!" he shouted at the top of his voice. "It's an attack!" A bugle call rang out. The Rajput warriors dashed out of the palace, carrying their weapons and yelling at the top of their voices. They hurled boulders and poured boiling fat down on the heads of the enemy. They fired cannonballs into the mass of bodies.

They rammed everything they could find against the mighty Jayapol Gate.

But the Moghuls outnumbered them. They advanced with the terrible, relentless force of a storm at sea. It seemed that they simply could not be stopped. "Look out!" came a shout. "They're getting through the gate."

The Rajputs rushed to meet them, keen to face the old enemy.

Bhupinder didn't know what to do. He stood with his mouth open, motionless. Through wide, staring eyes he watched as the battle raged in front of him. Arrows whirred through the air. Swords clattered and clanged. Horses reared and snorted. Arms thrashed. Voices yelled. . . .

Suddenly something caught Bhupinder's eye. He looked around and saw some Moghul soldiers clambering over the walls. In the heat of battle nobody had seen them scaling the battlements but somehow they had found a way over. And soon they would be in the fort and able to mount an attack from the rear. "Quick," he shouted. "They're getting in. Follow me." Picking up a sword, he dashed across the courtyard to confront the enemy.

Bhupinder was no longer a poor schoolboy from Nantapur. Now, all at once, he felt fearless and fierce, inspired and invincible. He felt as if he had been taken over by some sort of spirit. As if his body was no longer his own. He fought as if he was possessed, lunging and slashing like a mad whirling windmill. Single-handedly he managed to keep the Moghuls at bay until reinforcements arrived.

And the battle raged on . . . and on . . . and on.

Finally, it was all over. The Rajputs had managed to fight off the Moghul attack. After a fierce struggle they'd forced the invaders back out into the desert. The fort was safe – for the time being at least.

Still bruised and bloodied from battle, the Rajput warriors turned to Bhupinder. "Thank you! Thank you!" they shouted. "You saved our fort. If it hadn't have been for you, they would have caught us napping." They moved closer, wanting to shake Bhupinder's hand and offer him a suitably expensive reward.

After all, he had saved their fort. Not just once, but twice.

But suddenly Bhupinder didn't want to be a hero any more. With the battle over he snapped out of his warrior trance. One battle was sufficient. He had seen enough blood and death. He wanted to get away. To be safe . . . to be back in Nantapur. "If only I could be at home," he prayed. "I'd never call it boring again!"

Looking around, he spotted a narrow passageway. He started to run down it as fast as he could. His bare feet made padding sounds as he sprinted over the bare stone. The passage took a sharp turn to the left.

Bhupinder slowed for the corner and then sped off again. He wanted to get as far away as possible . . .

Suddenly his ears twitched. He thought he heard a sound. Was he being followed? Was a Moghul warrior after him? He was too frightened to look around. He simply ran even faster. His head was bent low. His arms were pumping. He felt that he had never run so fast in his life. It was as if he was floating over the ground.

His heart was thumping. He had stitches in his sides. His throat was dry. He could hardly breathe. But there was no way he was going to stop . . .

He tried to run even faster. But his legs felt heavy. His head rolled from side to side with the strain. He was at the end of his strength.

Turning a corner he allowed himself a quick glance behind him. He could see nothing. But there was definitely a sound. A slow, rhythmic padding which seemed to echo off the stone walls. Could someone be following him?

Bhupinder was scared. His mind raced with all sorts of terrible thoughts. What would the Moghuls do if they caught him? They'd surely kill him for stopping their attack. Would he ever see Nantapur again? Would he even live to see tomorrow?

Chapter Six

Turning once more, Bhupinder set off to accelerate along the passage. But he was too eager. In his panic, he stumbled and lost his footing. His legs crumpled under him and he fell in a heap. Too horrified to move, he simply sat still.

And listened.

He could hear the padding more clearly now. It was getting nearer.

And now there was also a swishing. Swish-swish it went. Swish-swish. Cutting through the air from side to side. "What can it be?" thought Bhupinder in panic. "Is it a sword?"

Slowly but surely the sounds came nearer. Pad-pad-swish-swish. Pad-pad-swish-swish . . . Closer and closer.

Bhupinder was terrified. He couldn't bear to look. He put up his hands to cover his eyes. He screwed up his face in terror.

Still the sounds came nearer. They were getting louder and louder. Pad-pad-swish-swish. Pad-pad-swish-swish. Pad-pad-swish-swish.

All of a sudden, the padding stopped. Only the swishing continued. Whoever or whatever it was, was standing right in front of Bhupinder. He could sense a large shape looming above him. He could feel warm air on his face. And a damp feeling against his neck.

"Any minute now," thought Bhupinder. "Any minute now he's going to strike."

He waited and waited. Still the swishing continued.

But nothing happened.

Eventually Bhupinder's curiosity got the better of him. He opened one eye and peeped out. Two large brown eyes were staring at him. He closed his eye and slowly opened it again. The large brown eyes were still staring. Who was it? What was it?

Using all his courage Bhupinder slowly opened both his eyes. It was Nandi! She was standing over him, her wet nose buried in Bhupinder's neck. And her tail was swishing rhythmically from side to side. Swish-swish. Swish-swish.

Bhupinder glanced up. Out of the corner of his eye he could see his brothers pointing and laughing at him. "Look at Bhupinder.

Frightened of a simple cow!" they shouted. Even Nandi seemed to be smiling.

Bhupinder ignored them. What did they know? He was the hero of Meherangarh. He had given the alert. He had spotted the Moghul soldiers climbing the barricades. Without him the fort would have been lost.

But now he was happy to be away from it all. No longer did he want to be a Rajput. He winked at Nandi. Perhaps making dung cakes wasn't so bad after all. And tomorrow he would be only too happy to play cricket. But he would never forget his adventures at the Meherangarh.

This is the market where we buy a lot of our food. Sometimes we bargain with the stall holders over the price. We spend our rupees on fruit and vegetables and sweets and spices. We put lots of spices in our food – it makes it very hot! We often eat special breads with our meals. I like chapatis. They are flat and round.

I like mangoes and bananas! Where do you buy your food?

We also buy cloth at the market, to make our clothes. The women wear saris or a salwar kameez. Salwars are pajama-like pants worn underneath a long, loose tunic known as a kameez. Men wear them too. Some men, like my father, wear a dhoti. This is a piece of cloth draped around their hips and their legs.

Your Daily Life

What is your day like?

What do you eat for breakfast?

What clothes do you put on? Do you have to wear a uniform?

I don't have a school uniform.

How do you get to school?

I walk.

What is your classroom like?

What do you do when you get home from school?

Do you have any jobs to do around the house, like setting the table for dinner?

I have to do my chores.

Where does your family buy food for dinner?

We get ours from the market.

Do you have any helpful machines in your house like a dishwasher, a washing machine or a fridge?

We have Nandi, our cow.

Do you have any pets?

We don't have electricity, so we can't use any of these machines.

What is your home like? What is it made out of?

Do you think your day is very different from Bhupinder's?

Lassi

Lassi is a very popular drink in India. It's refreshing and very easy to make. Why don't you make some?

Ingredients:

2 spoonfuls of natural yogurt

half a glass of water

1 spoonful of sugar

ice cubes

fruit, lemon juice, honey (optional)

How to make it:

Mix the yogurt with the water.

Add the sugar to taste.

Serve chilled with ice cubes.

To make a flavored lassi,
simply add chopped fruit, lemon juice
or honey and mix in.

Coconut Ice

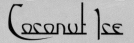

Coconut ice is a delicious Indian sweet.
And it's not difficult to make.

Ingredients:

1 small can of condensed milk

14 tablespoons of sieved icing sugar

a few drops of red food coloring

half a cup of desiccated coconut

How to make it:

Mix together the milk and icing sugar. Stir in the coconut to make a very stiff mixture. Divide in half. Color one half with the drops of red food coloring until it makes a pink color. Shape the mixture into two identical bars and press firmly together. Dust a plate with icing sugar. Leave the coconut ice on the plate until firm. This may take some time! Cut into squares and serve.

While you're enjoying them, why not play a typical Indian game?

The game of chess was invented in India. It was first called chaturanga and was different from modern chess. Originally the pieces represented elephants, horses, foot soldiers, and generals: the four key elements of the Indian army.